Andy Takes Action

Story and Pictures by Valerie Lang

First Edition

ISBN-13:978-1496096517

Illustrations, story and layout by:
Valerie Lang
www.vallangink.com

To Peter, Alina, and Susan,
for convincing me that dreams
can be more than fantasies.

To my teachers,
for their endless guidance.

To my family,
for their constant support.

One day...

Ms.T asked her students,
"What do you want to be
when you grow up?"

Leo wanted to be an artist.

Val wanted to be an astronaut.

Isaac wanted to teach science.

"I want to be an action hero," said Andy.

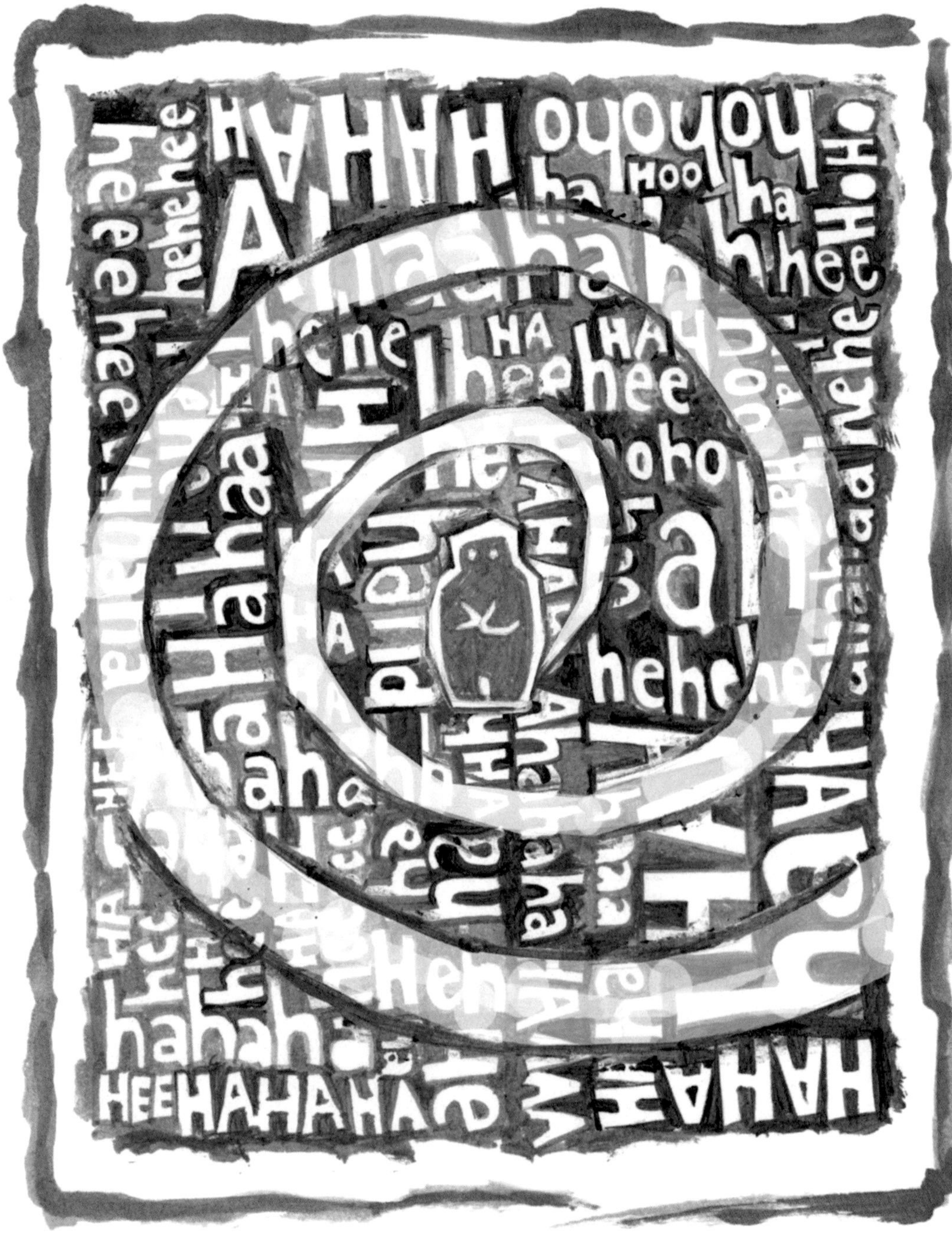

hahaha
HEEHAHAHA

But the other kids started laughing at Andy.

HAha
HOHO
hee

"You are not big enough!" called out Leo.

"Or strong enough!" shouted Val.

"Or smart enough!" said Isaac.

Andy felt ashamed for thinking
so much of himself.

Thankfully, Ms.T saved the day.

"Andy," she said. "You do not have to be
big enough, or strong enough,
or even smart enough.

You just have to be brave enough.

An action hero takes action...
even when it is tough."

After school, Andy hurried home.

He found his heroic helmet.

He donned a courageous cape...
and rose to action!

A

Andy started making a card
to help sick Susie Q feel better.

"Reow." Uh-oh. Andy's cat, Romeo,
was meowing outside the window.

Oh no! Romeo was stuck in a big crate!

"I will help you!" called Andy.

purr...
FRAGIL

Andy was strong enough, smart enough, and big enough to save Romeo.

"Maybe I really can be an action hero," thought Andy.

The next day, Andy found many more chances to take action.

In art class, Leo needed help
reaching glue in the supply closet.

Andy might not have been big enough
to reach the glue by himself.

But he was big enough to help.

In the library, Val needed help carrying a heavy stack of books.

Andy might not have been strong enough
to carry the books by himself.

But he was strong enough to help.

In the cafeteria, Isaac needed help figuring out how to split 3 cookies evenly.

Andy might not have been smart enough
to figure out the problem by himself.

But he was smart enough to help.

During recess, Andy climbed a tree
and watched over the playground.

He saw kids collecting sticks and stones,
jumping rope, playing tag, and throwing a ball.

Far across the playground,
he saw some kids laughing.

hehehee HAHAH hohoho HOHOHO

ha HOO ha

Ahaaahahh hee

hehe HA HAH heehee hehe

HA he hoho hao

HA haha HA HAH hoo ah ha

HAHA Ahaah h

HAha

HoHo

hee

Oh no! They were laughing at Suzie Q.

Andy wanted to help her.

But he was afraid.

Thankfully, Andy remembered Ms.T's words.

She said you do not have to
be big enough, or strong enough,
or even smart enough.

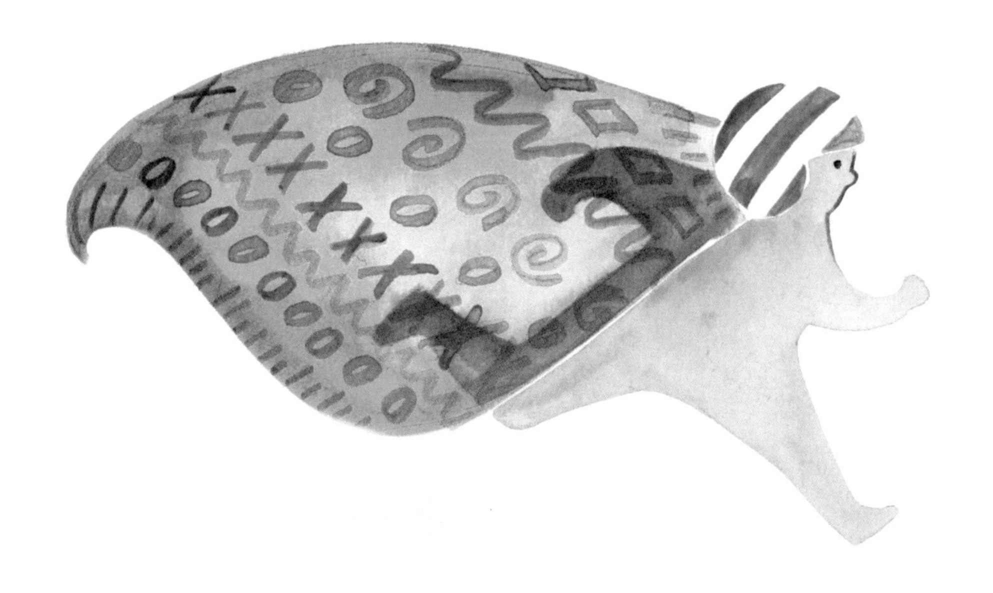

You just have to be brave enough.

Even though he was afraid,
Andy jumped in to protect Suzie.

He said, "Suzie Q might not be
As big and strong and smart as you,
But teasing only makes her sad.
Laughing at her, like you do,
Only makes yourself look bad."

The kids stopped laughing
and decided to leave Suzie Q alone.

"Thank you," Suzie Q said.
Then she asked, "Why did you help me?
Nobody else ever did. "

"Because," Andy replied.
"I am an action hero!"

“And an action hero takes action!
Even when it is tough.”

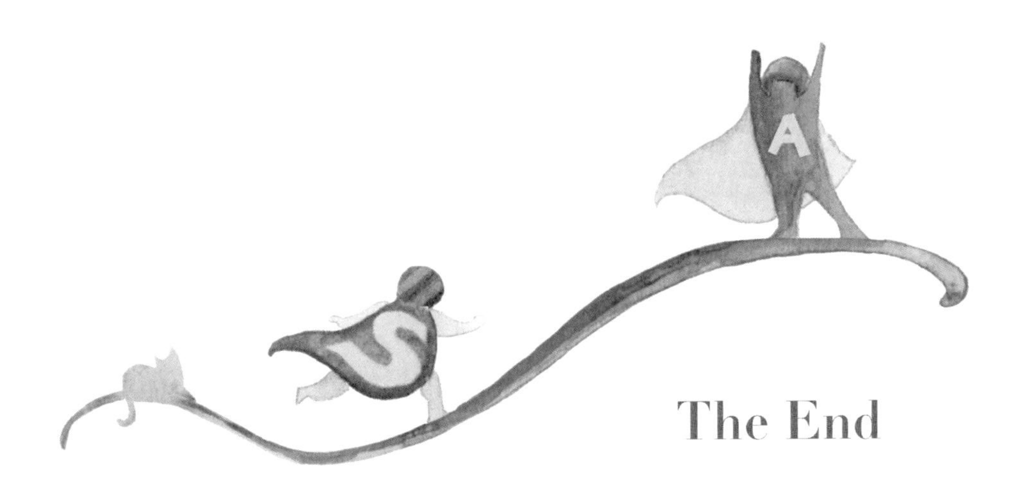

The End

About the Author

Valerie Lang attends Moore College of Art and Design, where she studies Illustration and Art History. She currently lives in Philadelphia, PA, where she spends half of her time working on art, and the other half longing for a cute dog. This is her first children's book.

To see more of Val's artwork,
visit: www.vallangink.com

Made in the USA
Middletown, DE
07 October 2017